PARDNERS

PARDNERS

©2015 Dale Lazarov & Bo Revel // All rights reserved.

StickyGraphicNovels.com

Printed and distributed by
ComicMix, LLC.,
71 Hauxhurst Ave. Suite B
Weehawken, NJ 07086.
http://www.comicmix.com

Printed in USA.

Hardcover ISBN: 978-1-939888-60-0

The
Guitar Pick
Music Store
Guitar Pick
Music Store
OPEN
4051
The
Guitar Pick
Music Store

The
Guitar Pit

4051

The
GUITAR
Store

The
Guitar Pick
Music Store
Guitar Pick

Marty, Your
Guitar Pal
615-555-51

LIVE
The
Guitar Pick

051
The
Pick
Store

Pick
Store

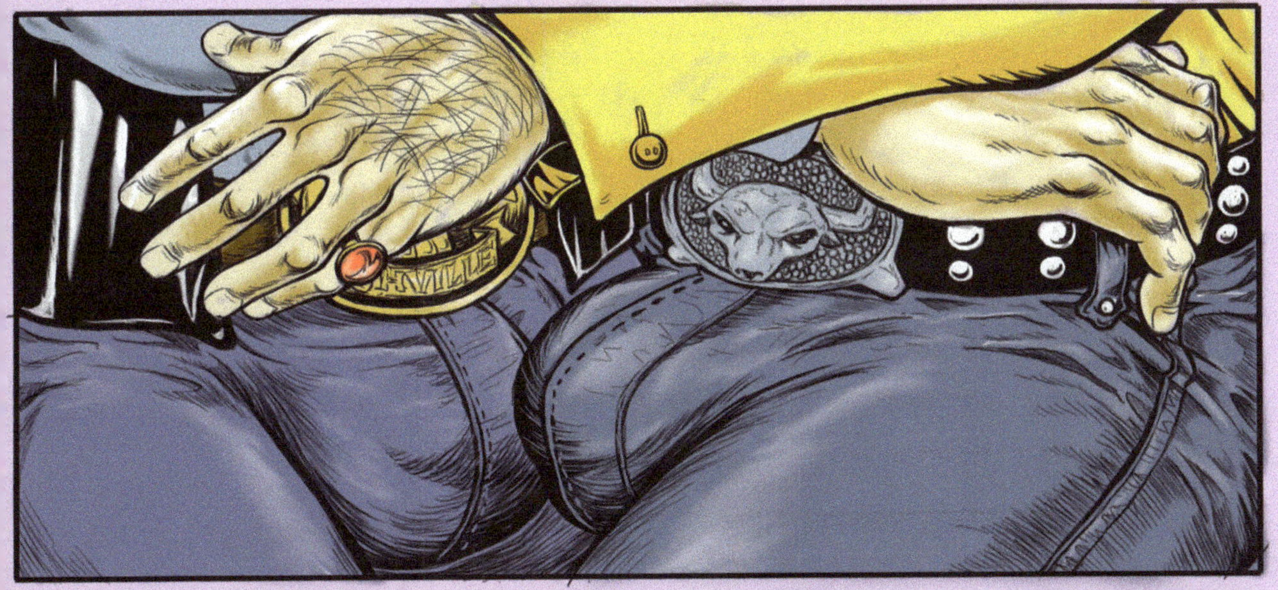

NASHVILLE

NASHVILLE

NASHVILLE

40
ur Pick
Music Store
CLOSED
Gone Fishin'!
Gui

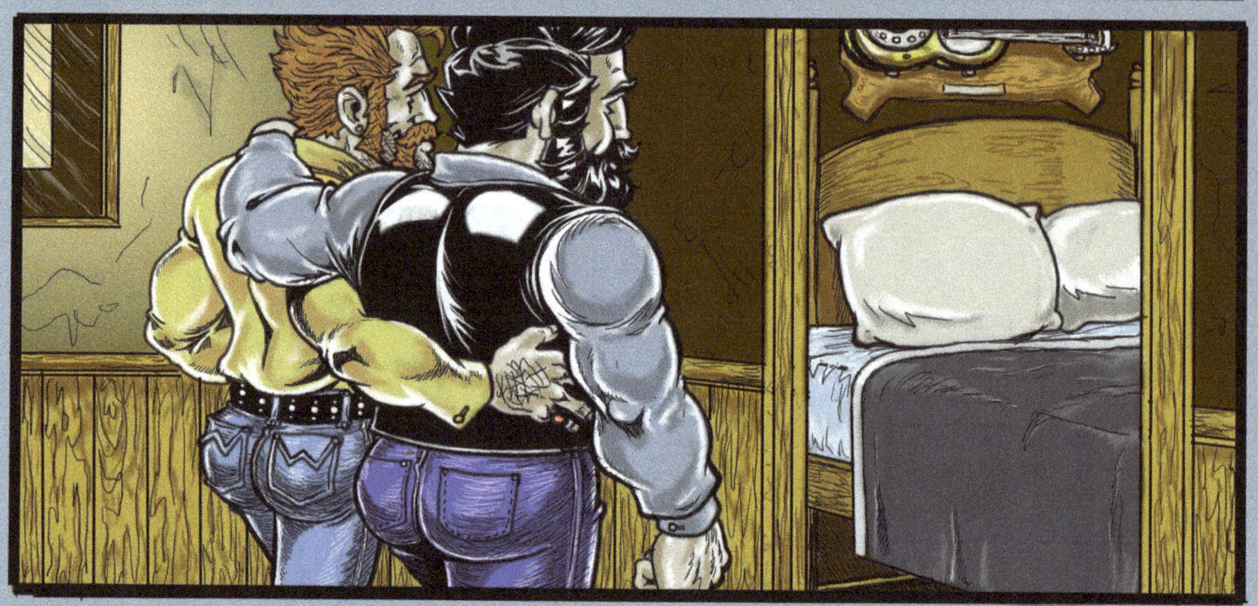

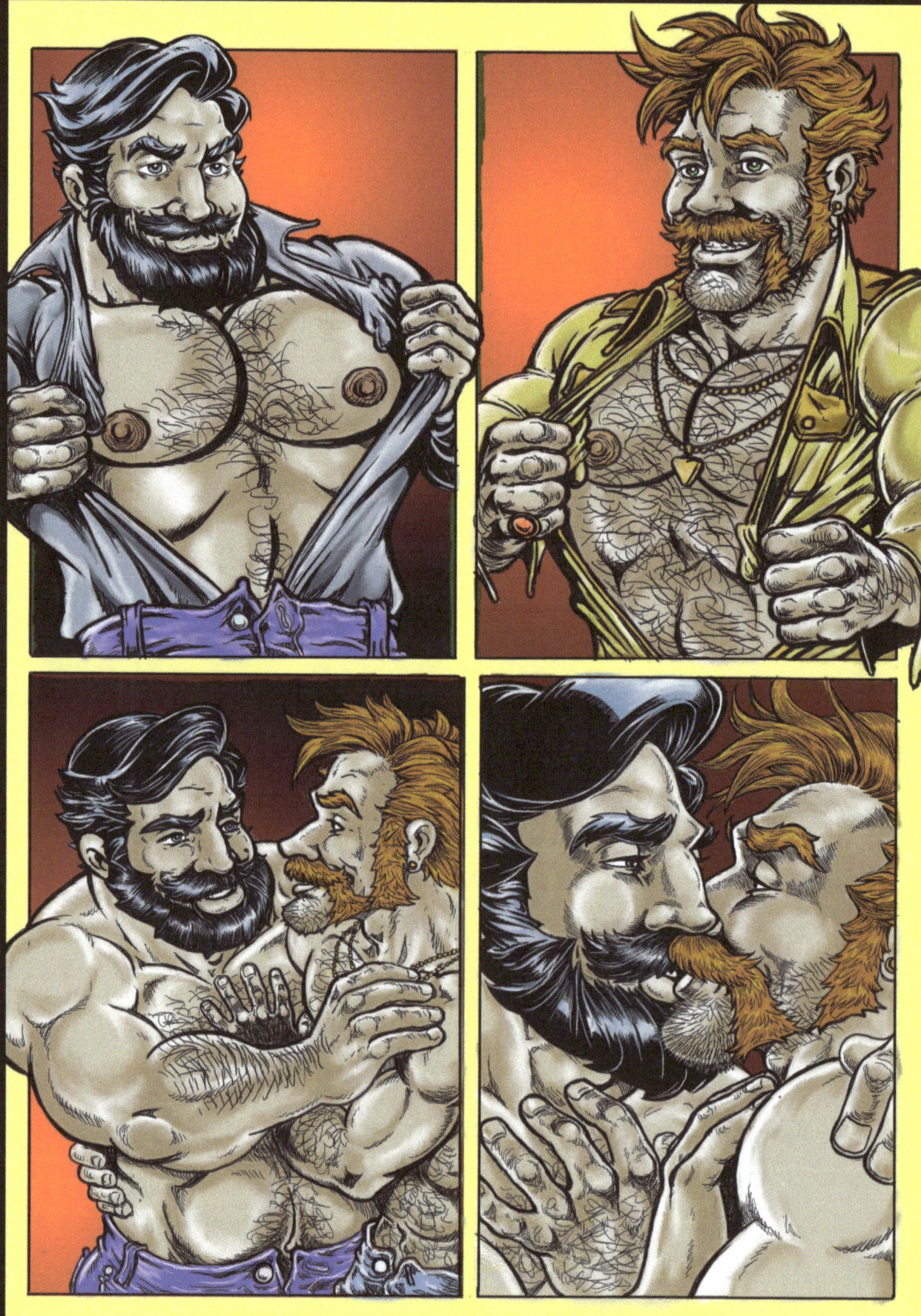

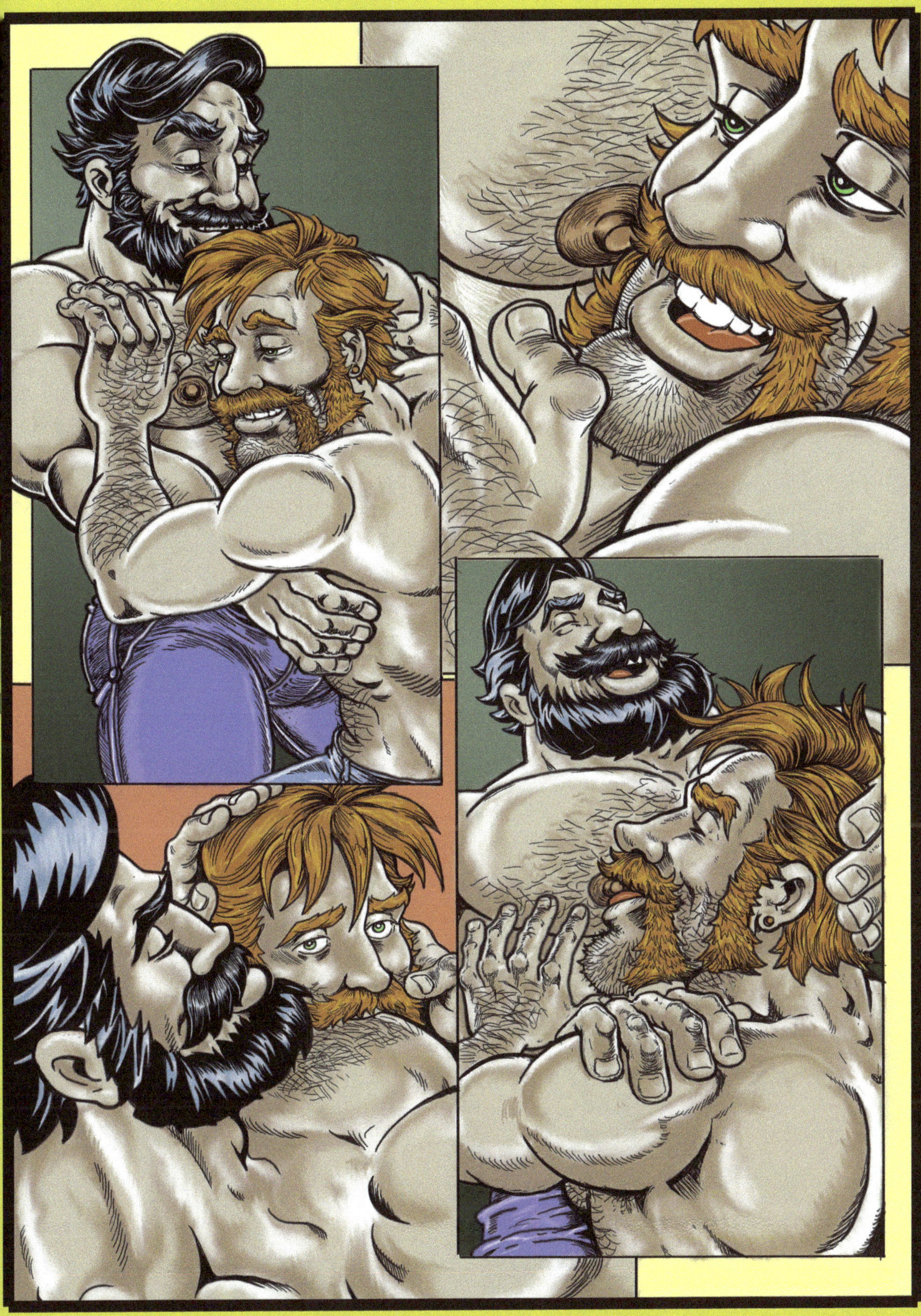

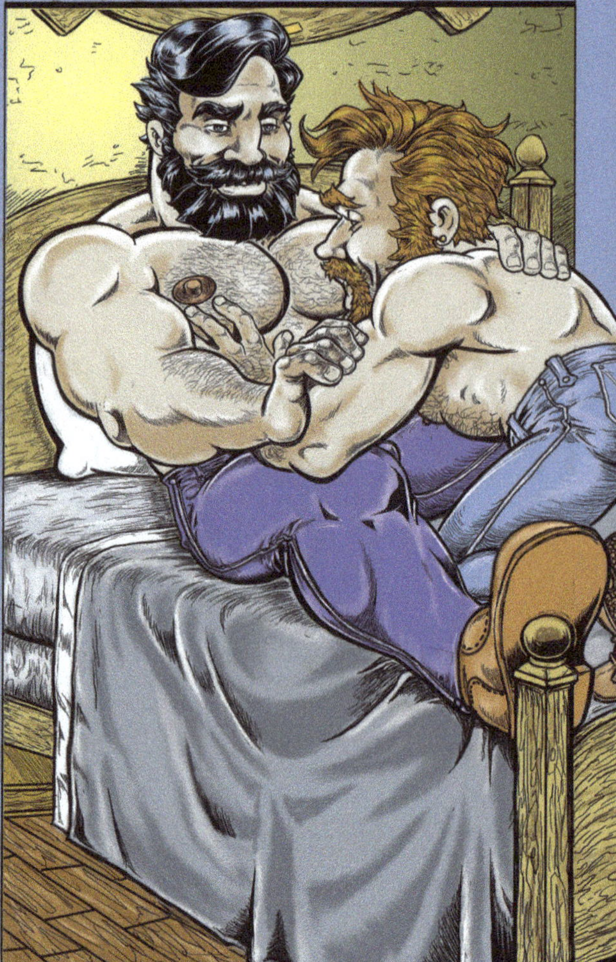
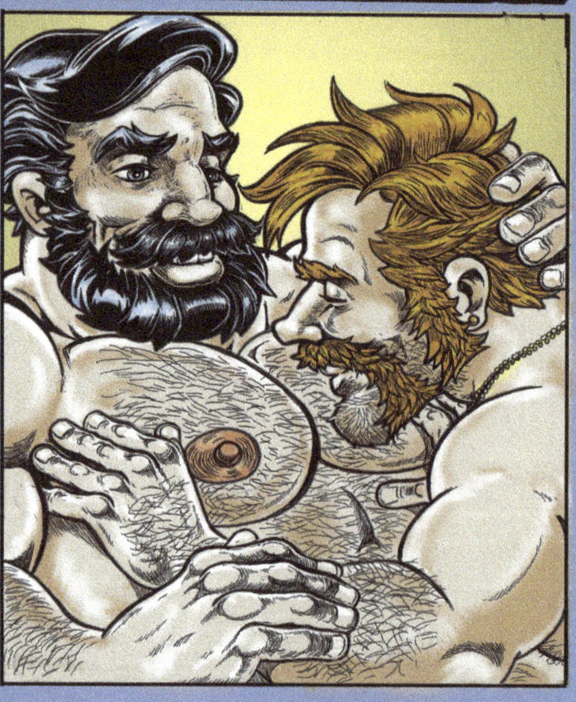

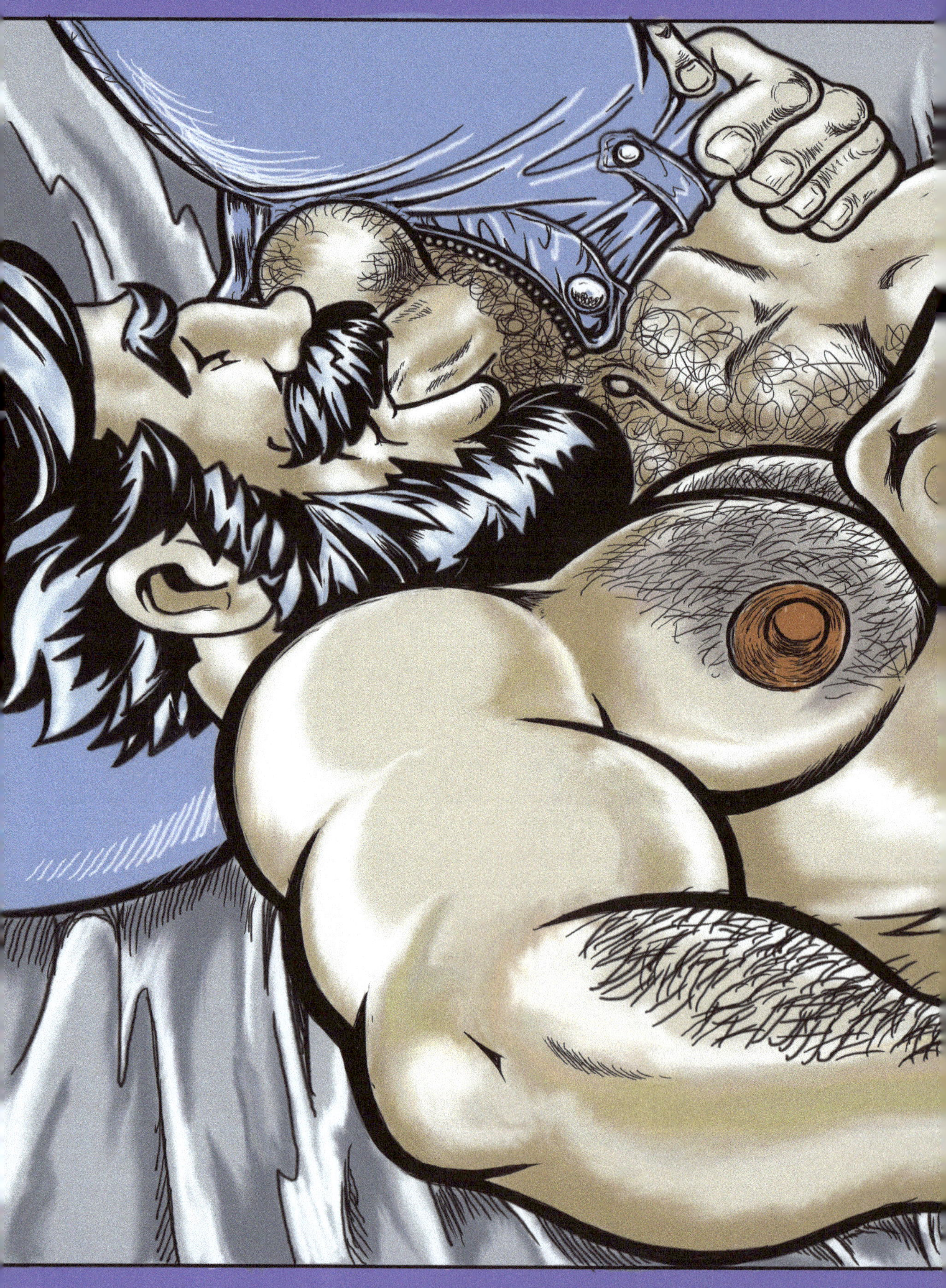

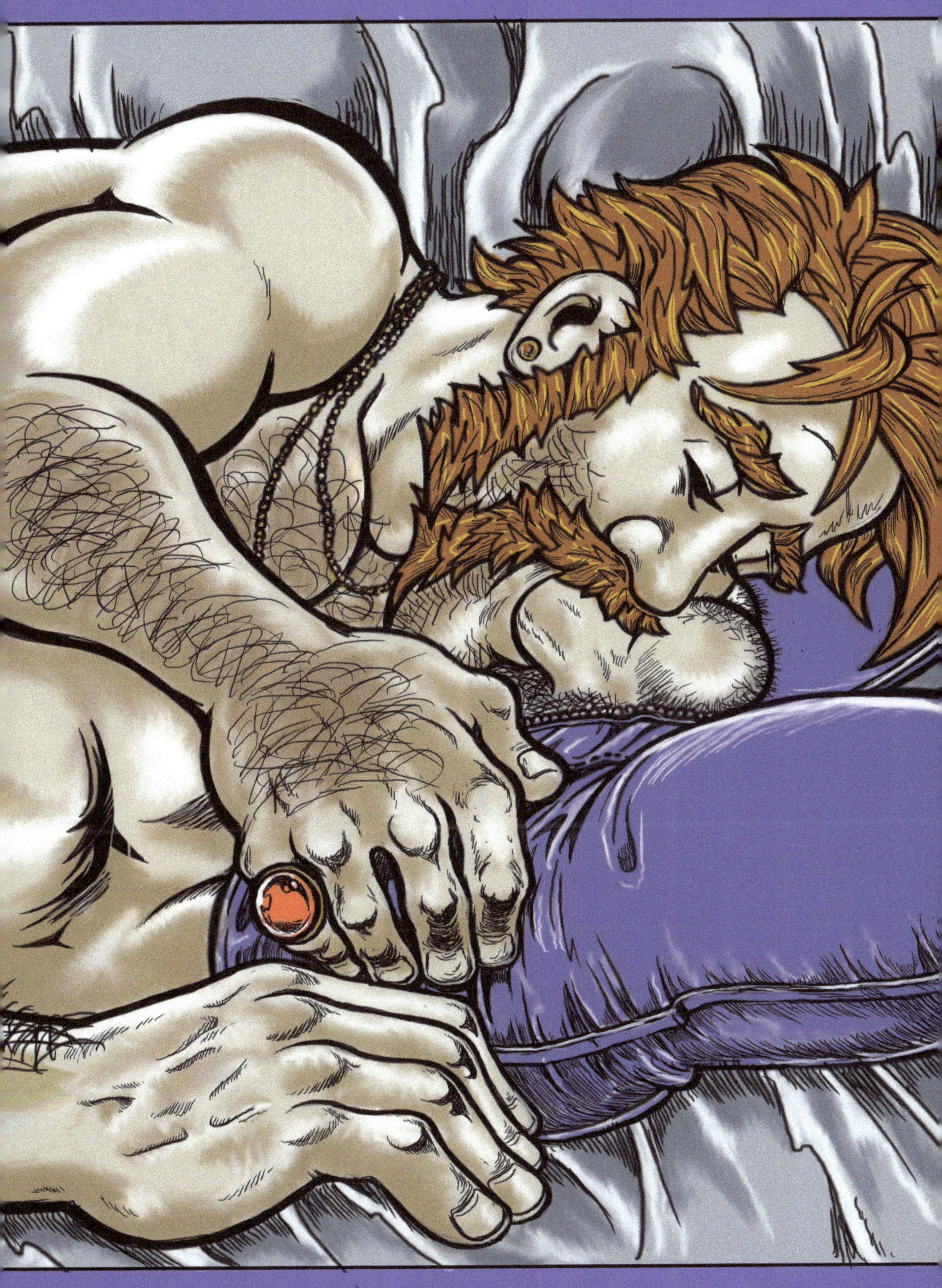

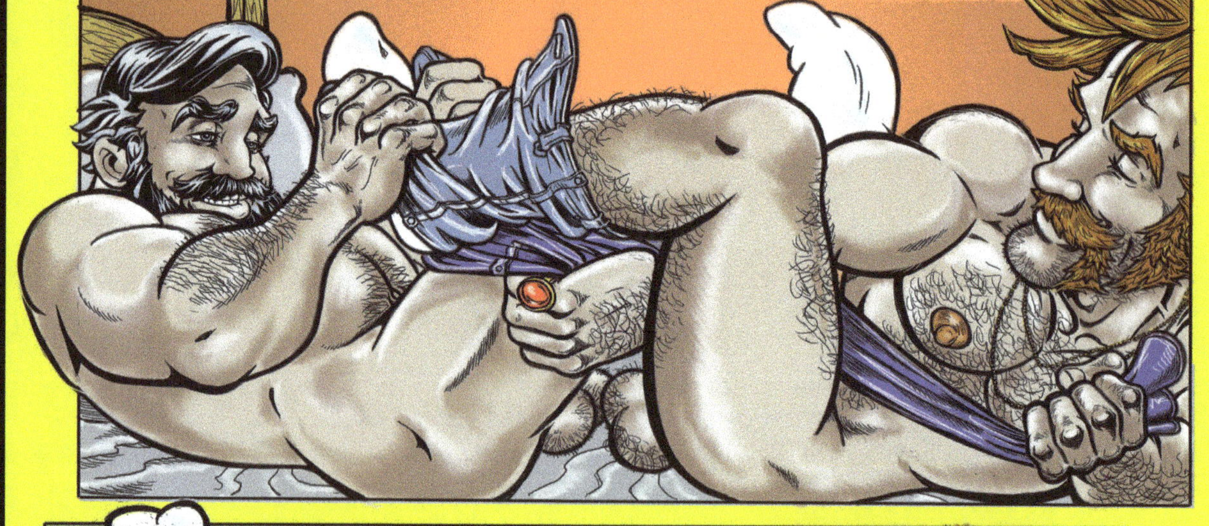
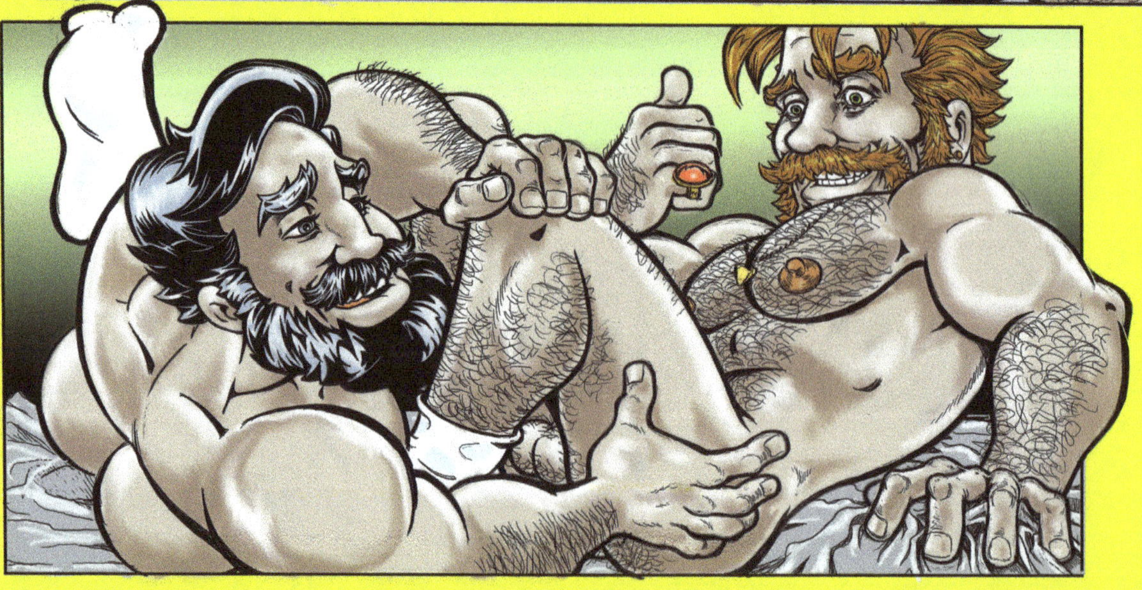

SM
SLI

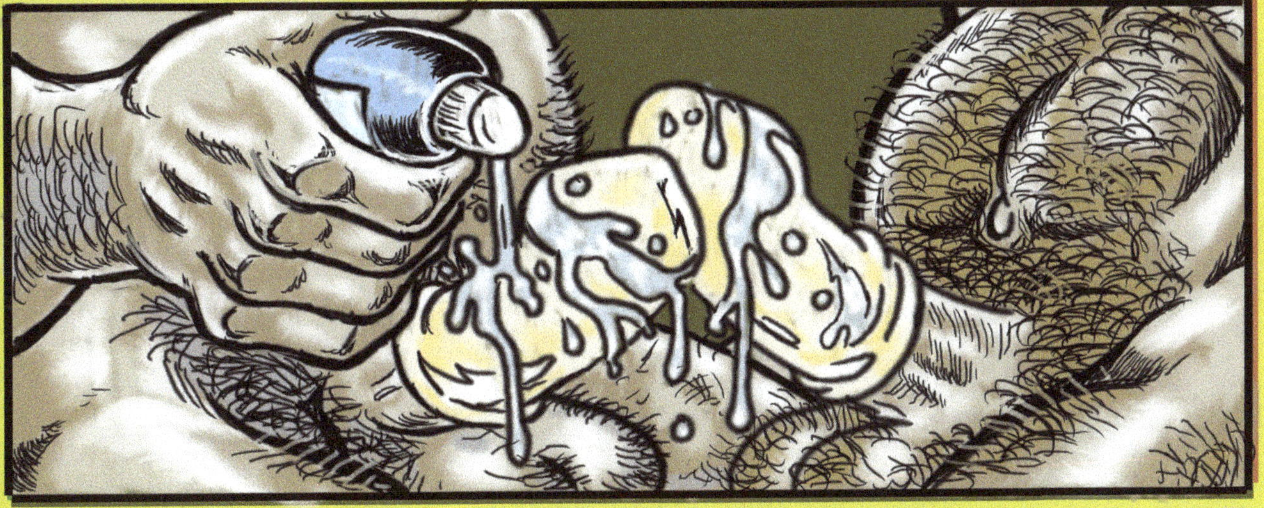

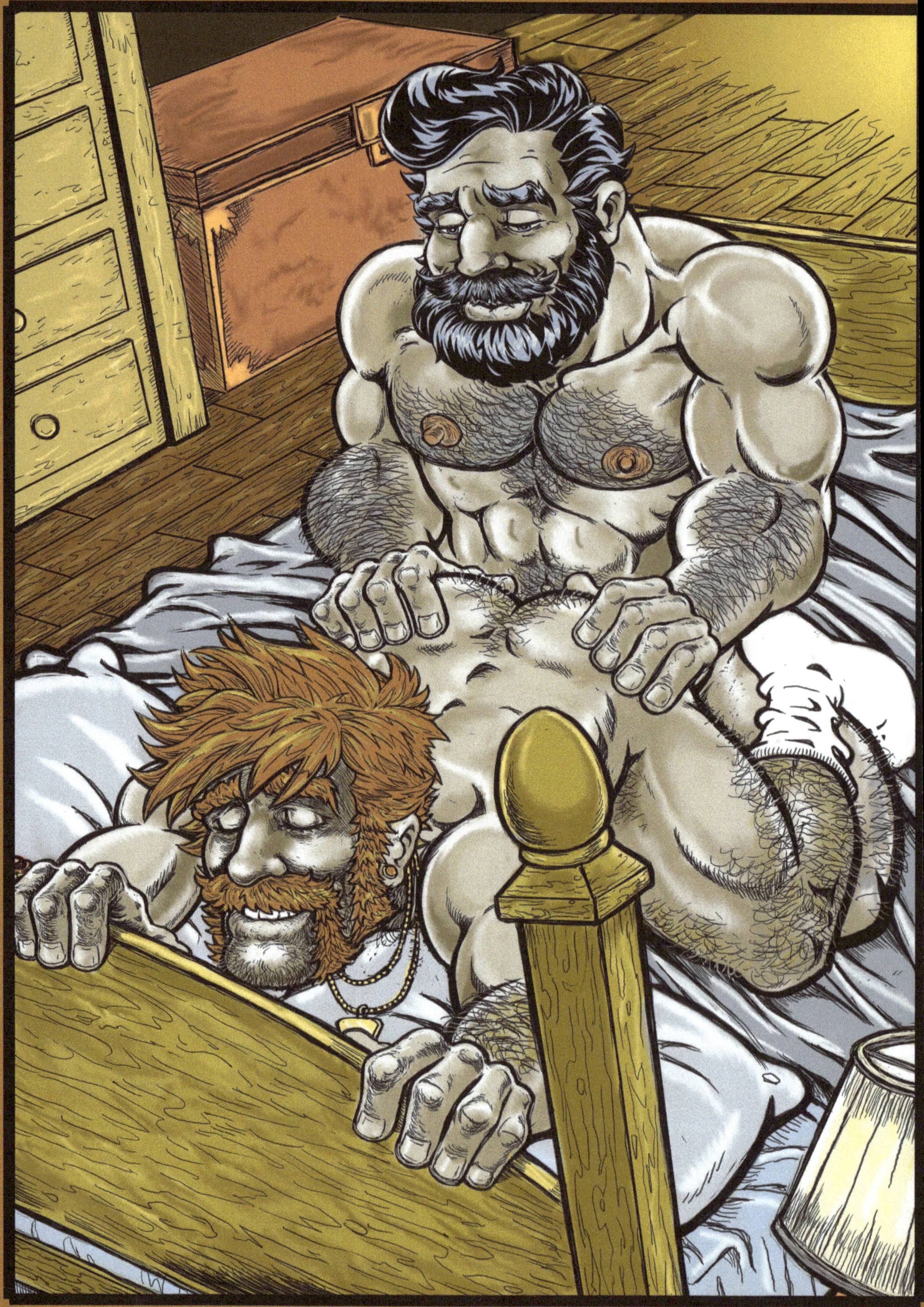

MAX
DL-47L
NU-CNTR-E
THE END

<u>About The Authors</u>:

<u>Dale Lazarov</u> is the writer, art director and licensor of Sticky Graphic Novels -- wordless, gay character-based, sex-positive graphic novels for an international audience. Since 2006, he has collaborated on 12 hardcover Sticky Graphic Novels and 39 digital editions with distinctive and evocative gay comics artists from around the globe. He lives in Chicago.

Like PARDNERS' protagonists, <u>Bo Revel</u> is a resident of Nashville, Tennessee. He has over two decades of experience in comic book illustration, portaiture, book cover art and logo design. Bo is married to his husband, Steve, and spoils his two cats rotten.

www.ingramcontent.com/pod-product-compliance
Lightning Source LLC
Chambersburg PA
CBHW041158300726
48981CB00004B/289